Signed Books and more:
www.mattshawpublications.co.uk

From the same author:

Captive Hearts
Chained
Octopus
Full Moon Trilogy
Nightmares

and over 200 over stories, all readily available on
Amazon!

"MONSTER"
The Motion Picture
Available to rent and purchase on Amazon now!

"NEXT DOOR"
The Motion Picture & Anthology
Coming Soon

With Thanks To The Following People

Rebecca Thompson
Jennifer Crawford
George Daniel Lea
Becca Ross
Jacqui Saunders
Gilly Adam
Melissa Kazas
Sophie Hall
Billy Smith
Lauren Downard
Kelly Blyth
Kelly Rickard
Paul McCarron
Melissa Potter
Jennifer Burg Pelfrey
Carolyne Lain
Andrea Dutton
Daryl Duncan
Chris Peart
Ian Clayton
Mark Martens
Jon Vangdal Aamaas
Carol Hill
PJ Peterson
Peter Le Morvan
Corrina Sangster
Yvette Grimes
Julie Shaw
John Burley
Karen McMahon
Joanna Taylor
Caroline Simmons-Hall
Tammy Evans
Lance Kreigsfeld
Mason Sabre
Hollyanne Trombley
Anna Garcia-Centner
Angela McBride
Debbie Dale

Jennifer Eversole
Cece Romano
Joan MacLeod
David Greenman
Paul M. Feeney
Jinx Da Clown
Jessica Stewart
Amanda Allan
Marc Moore
Symone Hooley
Louise Turner
Joy Boysen
Jarod Barbee
Sue Newhouse
Victor Roth
Nick Burgin
Nigel Parkin
Stephen McGuire
Kieron Callow
Karla Rice
Kristy Lytle
James Crighton
Kevin Doe
Dean Setters
Amy Deegan-Jones
Amber Chesterton
Remy Oliver
Kerry James
Donna Cleary
Lex Jones
Alison Hardy
Tim
Claire MacGregor
Scott Tootle
Travis James Armstrong
Marie Shaw
Michelle Ehrhardt
Gemma De-Lucchi

For All The Support You Show Reading My Work And Following
Me On Patreon. www.patreon.com/TheMattShaw

Splattered Punk

By

Matt Shaw

Sadly people like this character exist in real life. They believe themselves better than you and I. They believe they are the top of the food chain and that we are here for their amusement to do with as they please. This isn't the case though. We are not here for anyone else. It doesn't matter whether you're a leader of a free world, a highly paid actor, a successful author, doctor, nurse, nuclear engineer or even homeless with nothing to your name but the stinking clothes upon your back. We are all human.

We are all equal.

Never let someone treat you as anything but their equal and, if they try, cut them from your life like the cancer they truly are.

Matt Shaw

Part One

The Set Up

Nate Nasty (stage name) couldn't help but to smile to himself when he walked into the room where the interview was due to be conducted. The small room, filled with only a chair for him and a seat for the interviewer, was a far cry from the rooms he *used* to be interviewed in before his reputation proceeded him. This room was so minimalistic that he couldn't help but feel that he was similar in *threat-posed* to Hannibal Lecter in *The Silence Of The Lambs*. He could almost hear the organisers panicking amongst themselves now: *Remove anything sharp, that looks expensive - get it out here, hide the television, are you sure we don't have a room without a window?* Nate looked at his manager and publicist, Steven Gibson and raised his pierced eyebrow. Steven shrugged.

'Okay,' Steven said before Nate had a chance to bitch about the lack of amenities, 'you ready for this? New album due out, and a tour - we got a lot riding on how today goes.'

Nate winked at him. 'Relax. I've done my homework.'

Steven smiled but it wasn't a smile which suggested he'd been reassured by Nate's quick reply. But then, with Nate's reputation, did it really matter if he did make a mess of what was to come? At this stage of the game, people surely expected it from him. Fuck sake, it was half the reason some of his fans tuned into his shows. It was less about the music and more about the spectacle. The messier and more out of control it was, the louder they cheered. Steven couldn't really say anything. This was a monster *he* had created.

'Just make sure you get the fucking dates in there.'

Nate walked over to the two seats and opted for the padded one. He was, after all, the star of the show. The interviewer should just be thankful Nate was in the same fucking room as them, let alone allowed to sit with him for however long this was going to take.

When he was comfortable, Nate said, 'I said relax didn't I? I've done my homework. Dates all locked in.' He hesitated a moment before patting down his pockets.

'What is it?'

'Got any gum?'

Steven sighed and reached into his own pocket. He withdrew a pack of gum and tossed it over to Nate who, with little effort, caught it with one hand. Given the stench of alcohol coming from him, had anyone else witnessed the catch they would have been surprised.

Nate sang, 'And the duck waddled away. Waddle, waddle. Until the very next day.' He laughed. 'Thanks. I'm keeping them.' He took a stick of gum from the packet and dropped it in his mouth. The rest of the pack was dropped into the inside pocket of his metal-studded leather jacket. Already bored, he turned his attention back to the poxy room. 'Is this really fucking it? You didn't bring me to the cleaning cupboard by mistake?'

In truth, Steven was surprised by the room as well. Especially as the interview was being done on behalf of one of the leading music magazines of the country. Nate had seen their press interviews before and they were always accompanied by photos of the meeting. The setting tended to be in some lavish hotel suite. There were usually drinks on a table to the side of the shot, or in front of the interviewer and interviewee. There were usually lighting rigs set up. This just felt *cheap*. But then, Nate did have a reputation: The nicer something looked, the more he'd fuck it up. The publication was clearly looking to avoid any expensive repair bills. You didn't get to "number one" without ensuring your costs weren't kept to a minimum wherever possible.

Nate pulled the sleeve of his tatty jacket up, exposing his watch. He sighed heavily as he asked, 'So where the fuck are they then?' Before Steven had a chance to answer him, he asked again, 'Are you sure we're in the right room?'

Steven checked his own watch. They had been fifteen minutes late for the interview, so he was surprised that the interviewer wasn't already waiting for them. Especially when he considered how clear he had been when he said that Nate *hated* to be kept waiting. *Whatever you do, don't be late. Really pisses him off.* Unless - who knows - maybe they thought it would make for a more explosive interview by angering him before they even started.

'Fuck it. Let's go.' Nate stood up but was quickly prompted to sit his arse back down.

'Just - calm down. I'll go and see where they are.'

'And make sure we're in the right room.' He tutted. 'Sitting in the fucking broom cupboard like a right fucking lemon.'

'I'll sort it…'

'Takes the piss,' Nate muttered as Steven left the room. The door clicked shut behind him as Nate continued to look around, unimpressed with his surroundings. This wasn't him anymore. He had worked his way up from being interviewed in shit-holes like this. This was him back when he had first hit the scene with his band. Now, with the amount of albums they'd shifted, he expected bigger. He expected better. Frustrated, and with his anger rising, he got up and walked back over to the one door into the room. With a closed fist, he banged on it. 'Come on! I should be fucking by now!'

Why in the fuck Steven had arranged an interview so close to the end of a show was beyond him. He knew the routine better than anyone. Get on stage (usually half an hour late, if not longer), scream out the fucking hits, throw bottles of his piss into the crowd, get shit thrown back, get off stage, hit the alcohol backstage as his coke was lined up for him and the queue of girls dropped to their knees - mostly in turn - to take his dick and balls in their mouths. It was a winning formula and now Steven was fucking with it. To make matters worse, he was fucking with it *for this*.

The door opened and a pretty woman in her mid-thirties walked in. She was wearing a white blouse and a tight-fitting skirt which ran down to just above her knees. With glasses perched on the end of her nose, she looked like she was auditioning for the part of a sexy secretary in some second-rate porn film; especially with the way her long brunette hair was tied up. Nate immediately forgot his cramped surroundings and cracked a smile, showing his nicotine stained teeth in all their glory.

'I'm sorry to have kept you waiting,' the woman said. She set her black leather laptop case down and extended her hand towards Nate who took it without hesitation. They shook.

'Good thing you're pretty,' he said, 'or else I probably wouldn't have forgiven you as easily.'

Nate winked at her and she turned away both from embarrassment and a desire not to encourage him. They'd warned her he might be flirtatious. Flirting was fine though, so long as he kept his hands to himself. She could take banter but the moment he went to touch her, she'd slap him right back down again and would most likely get the hell out of there - interview be damned.

Nate watched as the woman started to go through her bag. She pulled out a notepad first - tatty and clearly full of random scribblings. Then, she took out a pen and sat herself down.

'Magazine struggling?' Nate asked.

The woman looked at him and raised her eyebrow; questioning him without actually asking what he meant. To answer her in a similar manner, Nate looked around their surroundings and smirked before he turned his attention back to the woman. She played stupid and continued.

'First of all, thank you for agreeing to see me and saying yes to the interview.'

'I hope it helps with the magazine sales and you guys are able to get back up on top.'

The woman smiled. 'I'm freelance.'

Nate went to say something but paused, unsure of what he *could* say.

The *freelance* journalist continued, 'Shall we make a start?'

Nate couldn't bite his tongue. 'You're freelance?' He continued, 'So not only do we do the interview in this shit hole but they don't even send a real journalist down to do it? The fuck is this? A fucking joke? You know who I am?'

The journalist reached into her bag and took out a dictaphone. She pressed record on the small button situated on the side of the device and then set it down on the floor between them. As she leaned back in her seat she said, 'We can start with who you are. Not the band. You. In this interview we want to get to know you; the man behind the band. We want to expose the truth from the fiction…. I'm sure you know the stories about you. Well, we want to find out what is real and what has been embellished by third parties…'

Nate smiled. 'Believe me, love, everything you read is true.'

The journalist looked at him. She felt the hairs stand up on the back of her neck as she recalled some of the many stories she'd heard of him and his bandmates. Could they really all have been true or was he just saying that for some kind of kudos among his diehard fans? If it was true, he was the worst type of human imaginable. If it wasn't true… Why would he be so happy to brag about it?

Nate continued, 'Well - I'm here now so, fuck it, let's do it.'

Part Two

The Interview

The following is the actual interview between the journalist and band singer Nate Nasty. Names have been changed to protect the identity of the innocent parties. The facts are written as described by Nate himself.

*

The Black Room Manuscripts is an English punk-rock band formed in Birmingham, United Kingdom, in 2010. The group was founded by bassist and lead singer Nate Nasty, drummer Joe Neil, and lead guitarist Sid Plyers. The band is often at the centre of much controversy with lead singer Nate Nasty leading the charge in - what he calls - his ongoing fight against the establishment. Since their debut album was released, there have been many

interviews with the band, their music and the message they desperately want the government to hear. This is the first interview trying to separate the man, Nate (who is responsible for much of the band's extreme and antagonistic lyrics), away from the band in an attempt to find out who he *really* is and whether he *really* is as far out as the press reports.

Words: Carolyne Brown

*

Just Who Is Nate Nasty?

When I first walked into the small room in which I was to be interviewing Nate Nasty, he seemed agitated and almost aggressive. No doubt because we had arrived purposely late and left him, alone, in a small room with only a couple of chairs. The moment he saw what I was wearing (a white blouse and tight-fitting skirt), his attitude turned to one of a more playful nature. That is, until he found out that I was a freelance journalist and not one of the magazine's top writers whom, he presumed, should be the ones to grace him with their time and talent with the written word. I told him that I was there to find out if the stories about him were true or whether they'd been fabricated by the press, desperate to find an "entertainment story" for their feature. His response was to smile and inform me that everything I had heard was true.

Carolyne: You like the room we chose for the interview?

Nate looks around the room (a small box room). After an exchange we have already had, I know this isn't the type of setting he had been expecting and I can't help but feel I am already pushing his buttons but, for the point of this interview, we <u>want</u> to see his reactions to things he doesn't necessarily like.

Nate: Fucking lovely really, isn't it? Reminds me of when I was young, living with my mum. She'd lock me in this tiny room while she sucked on the neighbours' cocks in exchange for bits they'd nicked from the local shops, or for a rock of crack - whatever they had. My mum was a right fucking whore (he laughs). Looked a bit like you funnily enough.

Carolyne: The song "Fuck The Slag" was famously written for your mum and there were rumours you did an acoustic version of this at her funeral a couple of years ago. Is this true? If so, isn't that a little disrespectful?

Nate: Look - that woman inspired me to get out of that shit life. Watching what drugs did to her pushed me away from them and live a cleaner life but there is no denying she was a terrible mother and somewhat of a cunt, right? I don't remember if she ever said that she loved me. I don't remember if she even ever hugged me. I do remember her shouting at me, and even spitting at me when I caught her fucking a police officer who came to have a word about an alleged theft she was a part of. This cunt... He comes in the house all serious-like, supposedly with eye-witnesses to her stealing whatever the fuck it was and the next, I walk in and she's bent over the living room settee with him eating her pussy from behind. She shouted at me to get out, spat at me and… Him, this bobby on the beat…. He just got up and stuck his exposed dick right in her. With me in the fucking room, he just started banging her. Plus side, it shut her up from shouting at me. Yet you sit there asking if it is disrespectful for *me* to sing that song at her funeral. Being perfectly honest, I'm surprised she didn't ask for a casket with a cunt-sized hole cut in it so her "fans" could have one final ride on her, you know?

Carolyne: You mention living a clean life yet you're well known as being a heavy drinker. Don't you find that contradictory? For most people, a clean life involves eating salads.

Nate: That even a real question? And salads? Do I look like a fucking rabbit to you? You need liquid in your body to survive, don't you? Well alcohol is a form of liquid.

He shrugs and laughs at his own "joke". I turn the conversation back to the room we have chosen for the interview and tell him that we went with this because of his reputation of destroying the rooms he stays in.

Carolyne: You once famously took a painting off the wall of one penthouse suite…

By now he is already laughing.

Carolyne: … and you set it on fire before throwing it out of the closed window. The painting was a one-off piece of artwork, given as a gift, to the owner of the hotel. The owner didn't want it hidden away from people and wished to share it with the guests who stayed in the more luxurious of the establishment's suites. Is that really true and, if so, is that the most valuable thing you've destroyed?

Nate: Fuck knows. They say it was priceless but - for all we knew they were onto an insurance scam. Maybe they had some debt to clear and knew I would tear the painting down and destroy it. I mean - I done 'em a favour. It was fucking shit. Looked like they'd given an idiot a paint brush and told them to go to town. Anyway - they said it was worth a lot and apparently we're not invited back to their hotel any time soon but who gives a fuck? Went to their restaurant for a meal and - fuck me - the portions were pathetic. Ordered a steak and got a tiny bit of meat with a smaller dollop of garlic-stinking potato and - I shit you not - two slithers of fucking carrot. Pretentious pricks. But anyway - the most valuable thing I've destroyed in my life? That's a tough one.

He goes quiet for a minute or two and I consider moving the question forward when he comes up with an answer.

Nate: Probably my marriage (he laughs). Oh fuck it, wait, you said valuable, didn't you? (He shrugs). Fuck knows. You tell me. What is the most valuable thing that I fucked?

Since they first came about, there is a report doing the rounds that the estimated total amount of damage the band has caused is close to just under one point two million pounds. They have supposedly destroyed a fleet of vehicles belonging to a rival band, every hotel room they have stayed in (which has now made booking them an actual room anywhere nigh on impossible), they've trashed green rooms at various venues, purposefully smashed up thousands of pounds worth of musical instruments, had to purchase their own studio to record in after being banned from all in their local cities and that is just scratching the surface of their destructive ways. More worrying though is that their fans seem to relish this behaviour. The more the band break, the louder the fans cheer. The band is literally being rewarded for antisocial behaviour. Taking his word literally though, I move the conversation onto something else that he has reportedly "fucked".

Carolyne: Speaking of fucking things…

Nate: (laughs) Ooh! Talking dirty. I like it.

Carolyne: There are reports of you with numerous…

Nate: Oh yeah, I fucked them all. Funny thing is - before the band - if I wanted my dick sucked, I'd have to pay for it. Now it's put on a fucking plate, you know? I can't even go do the shopping without some skank coming up and offering to swallow. Not that I'm complaining… And why wouldn't I let them? I'm a red-blooded male and…

Carolyne: Do you regret your extra marital activities?

Nate: Why because my marriage collapsed when my wife found out what I was doing? (laughs) No. I don't. Ask me why. Fuck it. Don't bother. Let me tell you a little story of a young lady called Becca.

Part Three
Dirty Whore

Nate: Her name was Becca, not that I would remember it by morning. It was only weeks later that - out of the blue - it popped back to memory which was, in itself, fucking random. It was the end of a show and I'd pulled her out of the crowd - mainly because she looked like she could suck a golf ball through a hose-pipe.

Backstage, she greeted me with a smile on her face, a mischievous twinkle in her eyes and her cleavage out and - already, within the opening *hello*, she had my undivided attention and I knew that she was wet for it. My favourite type of groupie. You know, not much effort needed. A little spit rubbed into the cunt and them pleading to be pounded.

I mentioned about how she looked like she could suck dick? Well, I wasn't wrong. Never mind the fact the back room was full of the lads and their choice cuts - she was only too happy to willingly drop to her knees and pull the old boy out. Before I could double check her age, she had me in her mouth and tickling her tonsils like a fucking pro. I remember it vividly which - in itself - must tell you how good she was given how much I've lost to alcohol over the years. She did this hand movement though, hard to explain... It was like she was revving the fuck out of a motorbike though - and all the time she did it, she sucked hard on the head of my prick. I was so wet from her spit that her hand glided over me beautifully so it wasn't as painful as it sounds although - nothing wrong with a little pain. Anyway, all the time she's doing this, she is fondling my sack with her second hand. Tickling it with her finger tips and nails and occasionally her hand would tickle further round, you know... That bit between arsehole and scrotum. Well, fuck me, I didn't last much more than five minutes. I remember, when I made all the right noises, she actually went to move away, you know? Like - after all that work - she wasn't up for a shot in the mouth. Well, fuck that. When a girl sucks me off, she takes the load. That's my rule. I don't want it spat back over me, I don't want it running down her chin. I want to hear that heavy gulp as she fucking swallows it down. I want to hear her fucking stomach say thank you. So I grabbed the back of her head and I held that bitch there. I made her take the load and I kept her there until I heard the old familiar "gulp". Only then did I let her go. She fell back, gasping for air and wiping the back of her hand across her wet mouth. Her eyes were streaming and make-up smeared down her face but - she wasn't fucking upset. She fucking loved it and before you say that's me just imagining her loving it. Wrong. You know what she did? This sassy little cunt asked if I liked how she sucked my dick. I told her - obviously - yeah. It wasn't half bad and she tells me... That was just the tip of the iceberg. She promised me the fuck of a lifetime if I wanted to carry it on into the night.

In the limo back to the hotel, back in the days when we could still book hotels, she sits opposite me, right, and she opens her legs. She's wearing no knickers. Just shows me her cunt and a neatly trimmed bush cut into a landing strip. Without a word, she started fingering herself. You know, just playing with her clit. Circling it with her index finger before she runs it down her pussy… I can still hear that gasp she let out when she pushed her finger inside herself. One at first, then another, a third… A forth fucking finger. The whole time, this crazy bitch was just staring me straight in the fucking eyes. Now normally I am a one time a night guy. Well - you know - I can fuck all night but once I've shot my load… I blame the booze but, yeah, I'm pretty much done. That's why, if it's a tasty bit of cunt… I try and hold off from shooting so soon. You know, if they're worth it. Anyway… This bitch… She's there, sitting in front of me and borderline fisting herself and I am rock. Like fucking rock.

Back in the hotel, we fucked in every position you can imagine except missionary. That's a position for the wife and the last bit of cunt I want to be reminded of, when I've been with these bitches, was my wife. She rode me, I banged her in doggie, up against the wall… I ate her pussy, I ate her ass, she ate mine… I even had her on her knees, mouth open, having me piss over her face and into her fucking gob. Later that night, I even tasted her own as she squatted down over me and broke the seal, so to speak.

The first time I shot my load, it was in her mouth. The second time, I was balls deep in her arsehole. I can see it in my head - clear as fucking day - when I pulled out of her. Left the bitch gaping wide. There was a little fart noise which, I remember, made me fucking giggle and then she shat out a trickle of my spunk which ran down over her pussy. It was fucking hot. More so when she scooped some of it up with her fingers and spooned it into her mouth... My cum into her gob... My cum that had just been shit out of her dirty ring yet this filthy bitch had no stresses when it came to tasting a mix of the white and brown. That is fucking dedication that is. You don't get that at home with the wife. You get, 'Oh not tonight, I have a headache.' Or, you get, 'Can you sort yourself out this evening?' But no - these bitches that come home with me... They have no boundaries, no off-limits... Everything is open as and when I fucking well want it and you are asking me... Not just five minutes ago... You are asking me if I feel any regret to fucking away from home?

Let me put it this way... *You* have a choice, right. You have a choice of going home where your partner is waiting with his tiny little dick and his one known sex position. He wants to fuck you for five minutes, yeah? He wants to fuck you for five minutes and then he wants to cum into a condom and fall asleep in a heap while you are left literally gagging for it… Sneakily rubbing yourself off as he sleeps in the hope you can tease out a fucking orgasm. Okay… So that's waiting for you at home, yeah? Or - you can go out with your mates who have fixed you up with this fucking mountain of a man. He wants nothing but to satisfy you. He doesn't give a shit if he finishes or not. He just wants to pound you until you're screaming the fucking house down. That's it. He wants you drained of a year's worth of orgasms in the space of just a few fucking hours. But - once he is done - he wants to fuck off and get on with his life, yeah? You won't hear from him again. He just wants to please you and leave. You can then piss off back to your husband and his small dick and his safe, boring sex in the hope that he gets lucky one day and finds your magic fucking button. So answer me this, would you fucking regret climbing the mountain?

Look - we get one life and all these cunts who put in all these fucking rules… They're ruining it for us. Live a little. Explore. Experiment. Fucking have a blast. You never know when you're going to die and yet you're listening to some unknown cunt telling you how you *should* live your life. Fuck that.

"Fuck That" was the title of one of The Black Room Manuscripts' top selling singles. It was a four minute rant akin to how Nate just spoke to me now; basically telling the listeners that they're fools for listening to rules established by other people. We should - apparently - be in charge of our own destiny and our own lives and we shouldn't be forced to adapt our hopes and dreams and wants based on how other people believe we should live. The song climbed in the charts and - at the same time - there was also a spike in petty crimes. Whilst some of those arrested made reference to the song, the song continued to play until - finally - the radio stations banned it from air play causing it to rapidly disappear back down the charts. I was going to ask Nate how he felt about people committing crimes

and saying they were inspired by him to do so but - his bragging about his sex life reminded me of another line of questioning I wanted to explore.

Carolyne: Becca Ross. I believe that was the name of the young lady you were referring to.

There is a change in his demeanour. He knows.

Carolyne: Did it upset you to learn of her passing?

Becca Ross was found dead in her home. She went to the concert and spent the evening with Nate. The following day, she didn't go home although she did text her friends saying that she was well and just having a "detox" of sorts. Clearly she woke up regretting what had happened. Months passed. Police were called to her home where they found her body in a state of decay. She had died of an apparent drug overdose. Nate was taken in for questioning but there was nothing to link him to her - other than that one night they'd shared together.

Nate: (with a sudden smile) Of course it did. She was a great fuck. Who wouldn't miss that? She died of an overdose. Makes me wonder if she was friends with my mother.

Carolyne: Do you think the way you used and abused her could have led to her death?

Nate: You trying to fuck me off? Whore died of a drug overdose. I don't do drugs. I drink, fair. But she died of drugs, not drink. She clearly couldn't handle whatever shit she was pumping into her veins and it happened way after we fucked so how in the hell does that come back to me? I didn't supply her. I didn't feed her whatever she took and - more to the point - I didn't force her to do anything she didn't fucking want to do when we *were* together. She wanted to suck my cock. I allowed her. She wanted a fuck. We fucked. If anything - her parents should be tracking me down and fucking thanking me. Their daughter was obviously a mess and yet I, out of the goodness of my fucking heart, gave her a bloody good time before she went and fucked her life up.

Fucking used and abused? You want to do your fucking research before you come out interviewing people or else you'll upset some cunt and have them storm out, leaving you with nothing to type up in your shit magazine for your shit readers. Fucking used and abused! I gave her what she wanted - even when I pissed in her mouth and she swallowed it all down... She fucking wanted it all. What? You going to blame me for all overdoses? My listeners enjoy drugs in their down time - they take too many and die and that's on me too? Fuck you!

I knew the question was going to be inflammatory but this was the kind of reaction I wanted. The infamous temper of Nate Nasty and how he actually got his surname "Nasty". As a man he has no respect for anyone or anything and that includes his fans.

Carolyne: I'm sorry I should have phrased my question better.

Nate: A fucking freelancer. You get much work, do you? Guessing not. You stupid cunt. Cunt!

Carolyne: What about a Mr. Dean. M. Watts?

Nate: Who?

Carolyne: Allegedly he came up to you after a show. He saw you in a bar across the street from the venue and approached you with the hope of getting an autograph.

Nate: You know how many people approach me for that shit? And what? You want me to remember one? I don't even know if you told me your name but if you did, I've already fucking forgotten it.

Carolyne: You put him in intensive care.

Nate: Oh Dean! How is he now? Have you spoken to him?

Carolyne: We haven't spoken to him. I was just curious whether he should have phrased his question better to you?

Nate: I'm fucking lost.

Carolyne: The way he approached you. I was just wondering whether he angered you or whether you did what you did just because you thought it would be fun?

Nate: Really?

Part Four

He's Just A Dickhead

Nate: You must think that I am stupid. I know what you're doing. You're trying to show my bad side and paint me out to be a villain but, in doing so, you're drawing upon shit that is fuck all to do with me - like that whore's overdose.

Carolyne: Not at all, we're just trying to get your side of the story. We have all read about what happened to the girl. We have read about what happened to Dean too but, we never hear your side of things. I'm merely giving you a platform from which to speak.

Nate: Really? You get me angry with your dumb fucking questions and then, when I bite, you have the fucking cheek to ask if that is how I handled that cunt in the bar. Like he couldn't have possibly done anything wrong, could he? I just lost my fucking rag and bottled the prick, right?

Carolyne: Well we don't know, which is why I asked.

Nate: Of course it is. Well okay, you want to hear my side of the story? Fine. I bottled him. I took the glass I had been drinking from and I smashed it down on the edge of the bar. I even sliced my own hand in the process, requiring stitches I hasten to add. Then, I turned to him and I jabbed that broken glass forward so fast and deep into his face that it ripped through his pretty little face with ease. And, not only that, I blinded the cunt too. Yep. That glass sliced through his cornea like a hot knife through butter, or whatever the fuck cliché you want to use. He fucking screamed so loud as he fell back, blood gushing down his face, tatters of flesh hanging from both his contorted face and even dangling from what was left of the glass in my bleeding hand. Thank fucking God for who I am though, right? I mean - had I just been a fucking "normal" like you then I would never have got away with just a huge fine. I would have got prison time. Although let's be honest. Prison for people like me isn't as bad as prison for people like you so - I'm sure I would have coped just fine but, even so… Harder to make my music when locked behind bars.

There is a silence between us as I wonder if he is going to add anything further. When it is clear he is done, I press on.

Carolyne: And that's all that happened?

Nate: What else do you need to know? You told me he came up looking for an autograph and I bottled him and he ended up in hospital, right? There's a beginning, a middle and an end.

At this point he pulls a packet of cigarettes from his pocket and takes one from the pack. I consider telling him the building is a non-smoking environment but, knowing him, he would still just spark up regardless. In fact - from what I know of him, if I were to complain, he would spark a further two cigarettes up and, worse, would do so with a smile on his face.

Nate: It's actually scary.

Carolyne: What's that?

Nate: How fucking stupid all you cunts are.

Carolyne: Would you care to elaborate on that?

Nate: Not really. You're all so fucking dumb I don't think I'd have the time to explain it in such a way you'd understand. Now - you want to carry this fucking interview on so we can finish up and I can go back to getting my balls sucked.

Carolyne: You take offence at some of the questions and are quick to anger but then you talk about *getting your balls sucked*. So on one hand you're offended that it might be suggested you live a different sort of life to normal people but on the other hand, you're almost coming across as proud about how you treat people. Like these aren't real people, just posh fuck toys for your pleasure only. It's very contradictory, don't you think?

Nate: Like I said, you're just trying to show my bad side. Maybe you want to turn listeners away from me, maybe you don't care about the aftermath of such an interview? Maybe you just want to sell your little magazines and get more subscribers because you're so cool and fucking edgy? Who knows.

Carolyne: You're wrong. I mean I have a lot more to talk about with you but I'm not sure if you're going to make it through the interview without storming off and, if you do that, we both lose. You get less press and we lose out on a story and being able to help….

Nate: Help? You think this sort of shit fucking helps me? Or that I need your fucking help? Lady, I am doing very fucking well without your help, thanks.

Carolyne: I'm not talking about helping you. I'm talking about helping them.

Nate: Them?

Carolyne: Society? The people? The world? People? Whatever you want to call them…

Nate: Fucking hell. What in the actual fuck are you talking about? You crazy fucking bitch.

Carolyne: We have spoken about just two things. We talked about a woman you openly call a whore, despite the fact she is now deceased, and you seem almost proud of the fact you bottled a fan and put him in hospital, just because the mood took you. There is so much more written about you though; none of it flattering or pleasant. My goal was to go through all of this with you but, with your temper, I believe you may storm out of the interview way before then.

Nate: And you wouldn't be wrong.

Carolyne: But then we wouldn't have the whole story for everyone. They'll read what little we have got with you, probably laugh about it and - from there - move on. They won't see why we had to do what we did and, for this to work, we need them to see *who* you really are. What a piece of shit you really are and why it's not a problem when you die. They shouldn't grieve you, they shouldn't celebrate you. They should just think of you as the idiot you were.

Nate: Fuck you.

[NOT PRINTED]

Carolyne: We need them to see that we did them a favour. We helped them by getting rid of you. Eliminating you from the gene pool.

Nate: Eliminating me from the gene pool?

I reached into my bag and pulled out the dart gun we had used time and time before. Kurt Cobain was shot with it, before his suicide was staged, as were Sid Vicious and Michael Hutchence to name just a couple more. Nate was just another entry on an already impressive list. He looked shocked - more so when the dart hit him and imbedded into his skin.

Part Five

A Different Way

Carolyne's voice mumbled into Nate's consciousness as - slowly - he started to come back around from the drugs.

'They're scum. These people. They're a plague to society as they go around making it seem *cool* to take drugs or that is acceptable to treat women - or men - as pieces of meat for their amusement only. They influence other people into acting the same way.'

Nate opened his eyes. Panic set in immediately as he found himself lying on a rubber mattress on an operating table. The walls were covered in plastic, the floor was equally covered. He was bound to the table with black leather straps, buckled in tight. In his mouth, secured around his head, a ball gag stopped him from being able to cry out or even speak anything other than broken mumbles. Carolyne stood before him. She was no longer wearing the "sexy secretary" look or rather, if she was - it was hidden beneath her protective overalls.

Carolyne leaned down to Nate and continued, '*You are influencing other people into acting the same way. And that, we simply cannot allow.*'

Nate tried to speak through the gag but, unsurprisingly, the words didn't come out.

'Oh sorry, was there something you wanted to say?' She added, 'The thing is, we don't need to hear what is on your mind now. We have enough from this interview to show people how quick you are to lose your temper. We have enough from *old* interviews to show them what a shit person you are. Certainly not someone to be thought of as a role-model. Certainly not someone to be missed. To think, before I put you to sleep, I was actually worried we wouldn't have enough to paint the picture needed but,' she laughed, 'we most certainly do.'

She sat on the only stool in the room, close to where Nate lay bound to the bed. She patted his chest and told him, 'This is how it is going to happen. Tonight, you are going to die. You poor man, struggling with alcohol and your demons... Jumped off a balcony. One of those deaths where people aren't sure whether you actually meant to kill yourself or if you were just so drunk you were being an idiot and slipped. Either way, a warning to others to not get as drunk.'

Again, Nate tried to speak but his words were unheard.

Carolyne looked at him disapprovingly. 'You had your chance to talk,' she said, 'and you decided to use that time to be an unpleasant shit. If it makes you feel any better,' she added, 'you won't have that much life left with which to regret that decision. In fact, speaking plainly, you have very few hours left of your life with which to regret anything and - you'll be pleased to know - you'll be unconscious for a bit of that whilst we get you into position for your oh-so-tragic accident.'

From somewhere behind the plastic sheeting, an intercom crackled. 'Carolyne, can you please pop out here for a minute?' The voice belonged to a male, unrecognised by Nate.

Carolyne made a *tut* noise at the back of her throat. Annoyed at being disturbed, she stood up from the stool and quietly left the room as instructed. The moment she did so, and Nate heard the door click shut behind her, he started wriggling against the heavy-duty restraints, rocking his body from side to side. Unsurprisingly, they weren't going to budge but then why would they? He wasn't the first person to be put in this situation and - by now - they'd got the technique down perfectly.

Through the gag, pointlessly, Nate tried to scream out - both for help and out of frustration.

*

Outside the room, the corridor of the otherwise abandoned building was more bare than the room Nate had found himself in. There was no plastic sheeting. The floors were made up of cracked concrete, the walls had holes and peeling paint with webs dangling here and there and yet - standing bold as brass in the centre of the corridor, there was a well-dressed man; suited and booted as though he'd come straight from a posh office block. Partially hidden behind a thick beard, he was smiling broadly in Carolyne's direction.

'Change of plans,' he said, the moment she stepped out of the room. 'I trust I'm not too late?'

'Of course you aren't.'

'As in - he is still conscious?'

'He is still very much conscious.'

The suited man's smile widened. 'Excellent.' He continued, 'Well, as I said, there has been a change of plans from the client. One we cannot afford to ignore.'

Carolyne bit her tongue. The company had got away with this for so long because their plans were meticulously thought out. Nothing was left to chance. The moment plans were changed at the last minute was the moment things had a greater opportunity of going wrong. And when something like this went wrong, it wasn't just a question of a company going under. It meant *prison-time.*

'We are going to have the last interview with Nate Nasty before he is found brutally murdered. Tortured to death, in fact.'

Carolyne looked confused. She wasn't able to bite her tongue anymore and said, 'How will that teach people a lesson?' She added, 'The plan we have... He has alcohol in his system, he jumps or falls… People know not to over-drink… People read the interview and just see him as an idiot and that he isn't worth mourning. That was the route of the article.' She continued, 'If he is tortured to death…' She shook her head. 'I don't think this will go the way we were planning.'

'Yet it is what we are doing. Now if you have a problem with that we can remove you from this assignment and place you elsewhere, when something else comes up, but that does mean you forfeit any monies already owed for your hard work.'

'I didn't say I won't do it…'

'And we know you don't like blood on your hands… Well, literal blood. So I have taken the liberty of calling in a team to help you with the torturing so… Where you go next is down to you. You can go back to the room and await the team's arrival or you can leave the building now and await contact for a new assignment.' He pushed her for an answer, 'Which is it to be?'

'When have I ever backed out of a task?'

The bearded man smiled and nodded. 'Good for you. Well, you go and keep him company and the team will be in with you soon, okay?'

Carolyne nodded. Without waiting for him to give further instruction, she about turned and headed back to what was now going to be the torture room. The suited man watched her for a moment, nodded again and then he himself headed back down the corridor from whence he first came.

*

The clicked shut behind Carolyne as she approached where Nate lay on the operating table. She calmly took a seat upon the stool she'd previously been sitting on and quietly informed him that, 'Plans have changed. Trust me when I say this is a most peculiar turn of events because once something is set in motion, that tends to be it. There are no reprieves and there are no changes. We stick to the plan, we pull it off in a professional and flawless manner and we put the matter to bed.' She paused a moment. 'I can't tell you I am particularly happy about this but you know how it is. We get our instructions from the top and whether we believe in them, or not, we have to go through with them. What was it they said? The man kicks the dog, the dog bites the cat, the cat eats the mouse. In case you're wondering - in this case - you are the mouse, I am the cat and my boss is the dog. There is, of course, someone above him but really, none of this is important.' She took a breath. 'What you need to know is, the plans have changed. You will not be thrown from a high-rise now.'

Despite the ball-gag, Nate still managed to breathe a sigh of relief. Carolyne smiled at his response. Did he really think they were just going to let him go?

Carolyne told him, 'You aren't going to be thrown from a high-rise but you are going to be tortured to death. Knowing the team coming to take care of you, I am one hundred percent sure you'd prefer to have been thrown from the top of a building. From what I am led to believe, the death is usually instantaneous. This… Well this *won't* be.'

More muffled and incoherent mumbles from Nate as he tried, unsuccessfully, to beg for his life.

'Don't worry,' Carolyne said, 'I am sure *they* will give you a chance to have your say. Until then, you might want to try and rest up a little. I believe we are both in for a long night.' She added, 'At least - that is what I presume for I have never *actually* witnessed a punishment such as this. It is as new to me as it is to you. Although,' she finished, 'I expect I have the better seat for this one.'

Carolyne laughed.

Part Six

Headed for Martyrdom

Nate wasn't aware of the concept of "time" as he lay there, groggy from whatever drug the bitch had shot him with. Ten minutes could have gone by, with only her and him in the room, or ten hours and he wouldn't have known the difference. Even when *they* entered the room, he barely registered the fact Carolyne and he were no longer alone and it had only really sunk in when they introduced themselves.

There were four of them in total. With Carolyne, it took their numbers to five. Just as Carolyne was covered in protective clothing, so too were they. Unlike Carolyne though, their faces were also covered with surgical masks and clear plastic specs protected their eyes.

'Good evening, Mr. Nasty,' one of them said in - considering where they were - a fairly polite and respectful tone. 'My name is Mr. White. I'm pleased to make your acquaintance.'

As Mr. White spoke, the three other masked strangers started empty bags they'd brought in with them, laying the items down upon the covered floor as though a table had been forgotten.

'I trust my colleague here explained what will be happening over the course of the next few hours?' He cast a glance to Carolyne who nodded in answer to his question. He smiled behind his surgical mask. 'Excellent.'

One of the crew pulled a tripod from within the bag which they proceeded to extend and set up, close to where Nate lay. With the tripod in place, they returned to the bag and came back with a camcorder. Silently, they set the camera up on the tripod and - with a signal from Mr. White - turned it on and hovered his finger over the record button, ready for the next signal.

Carolyne took a step back until her back was pressed against the covered wall. Whilst it was necessary for her to remain present, to ensure the job was done properly, she didn't have to stand so close as to get splattered punk all over her.

Nate's eyes were fixed directly on the camera pointing at his face as though he was trying to reach an audience of people watching, even though it wasn't connected to anything and the device wasn't yet recording. His look hadn't gone unnoticed.

'You're probably wondering about the camera,' Mr. White said. 'Well this is so we can film what happens to you. You see, when we're done with you and you're long since cold in the dirt - we're going to be releasing this tape to the media.'

Carolyne shook her head and stormed from the room much to Mr. White's surprise. Outside, she reached under her protective layers and pulled out her cell. Speed-dial 1. She started to impatiently pace as the call took its time to connect. Once it had though, it only rang once before it was answered.

'I didn't think it would be long before you called,' a voice said from the other end of the line. The same man who'd first pulled her into the corridor earlier.

'What the hell is going on? One thing to torture him but - we're going to release the tape too?'

'That's right.'

'This is ridiculous. You'll make him into a martyr. People will mourn him. People will hold damn vigils for him. You won't turn them away from him. You'll turn them to him! This man, so opposed to all that society says is good, making his own rules as he goes along - suddenly seen tortured to death for his beliefs. Even people who have never heard of him before now. This will be massive.' She continued, 'Do I need to remind you of *his* death? Instead of just making it an accidental overdose, the company turned *his* death into a suicide - leaving behind a note too. They sell prints of that note on a shirt. And - where his memorial is - junkies make pilgrimages just to go down there and pay their respects by shooting up. His death taught nothing. He is still a bad influence and a hero to the damaged and that is exactly what we are going to do with this guy.'

'First of all you know very well that case didn't go as planned. How were we supposed to know that he was so used to drugs in his system that the tranquilliser wouldn't last nearly half as long as usual. He woke up, he fought back, he was shot. We had no choice but to go down the suicide route of the rifle. Hide a bullet hole by making a bigger one. We made the best of a bad situation and *this* is not the same as that in the slightest.' The voice on the other end of the line continued, 'This piece of excrement isn't even in the same league as young Kurt was. Nate Nasty's reach is tiny and if it weren't for the deal, we wouldn't even be looking at him. Now, we have been asked to do this. We have been paid handsomely to do this. We *will* do this. As I said to you earlier, if you wish to leave now, you're more than welcome but this is happening.'

Carolyne hesitated, unsure of what to even say. He was right. In the great scheme of things, Nate Nasty was beneath them. Yes, he had a following. Yes, he sold albums. Yes, he did well for himself. He certainly wasn't in the league of some of their usual contracts though.

'I'm sorry, sir.' Carolyne back-tracked, suddenly remembering her place in the great scheme of things. 'You know I struggle when plans are changed.'

'As do we all but we do what we must.'

'It would just help if I knew the reasons,' she continued. Of all the cases she had been a part of, working with this company, she had never questioned them before and so wasn't sure whether her manager would even listen to her or whether he'd just tell her to get on with it but she knew, if she didn't speak her mind - it would only eat at her further down the line.

'All you had to do was to ask,' her manager said in a cheerful tone.

Part Seven
(BEFORE)
The Decline

The bearded man, whose name was Martin, sat opposite his new client who was busy reading the terms and conditions of the contract he was looking to enter into. They were sitting in a plush office in the good part of the town. Martin was staring out of the window at the world below, giving his client some space in order to not make him feel pressured into signing something he wasn't entirely happy with. Perks of an office at the top of the building was that the view stretched for miles and - every time Martin looked out over it - there was something new to see.

'Seems okay,' the man said as he turned the contract back to the first page. 'There's just one thing that bothers me.'

'Shoot.' Martin swivelled in his chair so that he was facing the client again.

'I sign this and basically I'm signing a confessional to what is going to happen. How do I know you won't just hand this to the authorities?'

'Let me remind you that you found us. You came looking for our services. We're not here to frame anyone. We are simply here to provide a service that others may frown upon, out in the real world. But let me assure you, we have full authorisation to target people such as the man you're bringing to us. The government turns a blind eye so long as we pay our taxes and give them a little kick back. And, if you think about it, a lot of the time we are doing them a favour. They don't like these people. They don't like the influence they have on the "normal" members of society. If they're wiped from the face of the earth, and painted out to be the villain at the same time - they're actually happy.' Martin smiled. 'If they weren't, we wouldn't get a Christmas card from them every year now, would we?'

'You actually get a card from them?'

Martin shrugged. 'We pay them a lot of money to keep them in the seats they hold. Their way of showing some gratitude, I guess. Now that being said, we can't go taking people out whenever we wish. We have to build a file, we have to present it to the powers that be and if they say we can't, for whatever reason, then - of course - you will have a full refund and your contract will be marked as void.' Martin explained, 'It is the process that everyone goes through and it ensures the wrong person is not

taken out. For example, what if you were here to get us to murder a scientist? Maybe he is part of the government's own plans? The government would decline the report. But, from what you're saying, you're here to have this Nate Nasty character taken care of and, well, I've read enough about him to know he is unsavoury. I can speak with some level of confidence when I say the government will have no issues in green-lighting this.' Martin smiled. He was used to explaining this to people such as this client. It was only right that they were nervous when presented with a contract which they had to sign, to prove it wasn't just the company picking and choosing who to have killed.

Martin leaned forward in his chair and held out a Mont Blanc pen with a golden nib. His client hesitated a moment before he took the pen. There was another slight hesitation as he looked upon the contract once more and - then - he signed. He replaced the lid on the nib and handed both contract and pen over to Martin who gladly accepted both.

'Thank you, Mr....' He glanced at the contract and read the man's name, 'Gibson.' He continued, 'We will of course get this counter-signed and sent off to the government officials before we contact you with regards to the payment. The whole process usually takes a couple of days. Sometimes it can be longer if the government needs to research the character but from what you have told me and what I know of this gentleman, it should all happen fairly promptly.'

Steve Gibson stood up and extended his hand. Martin stood and shook it.

'Thank you,' Steve said.

'Not at all. Thank *you* for bringing us your business.' Martin stepped out from behind the desk and led Steve towards the door. 'There is just one question,' he said tentatively.

'Yes?'

'You're Nate's manager so - why?'

Steve said coldly, 'Because his music isn't quite as popular as it once was. The tour he is due to go on - it's going to have a lot of empty seats and lose us a lot of money if we go ahead with it. That, in turn, will damage the next album. And given the lacklustre sales of his previous album… We have invested a lot of money into this *character* and have the potential to lose a whole lot more. If he is dead, we can offer special holographic commemorative tickets to those who had a concert ticket, similar to the ones they offered for Michael Jackson. Put limited edition on it and people will snap that shit up if only to try and sell on eBay. Even those who want a refund - we shouldn't lose too much money because his death will also drive the album sales up. His final album. People will flock to it in order to see if he'd at least gone out on a high. So - no more expense with having to put the concert on *and* a push in album sales. This is purely business.'

'I understand,' Martin said coldly. He *did* understand. This was how more than half of his business was conducted. It was never personal and always about cash. 'Well, we will be in touch.'

Martin walked Steve to the office door and held it open for him. Steve paused a moment and asked, 'How will you do it?'

'How will we kill him? We prefer not to divulge that information,' Martin said. 'Sometimes we figured it is best you don't know *everything*.'

'Well it's my money and I think I would like to know.'

Martin nodded slowly. 'Okay well, we will work out the details, once everything is approved and then we will, of course, keep you informed.'

'And remember - I really need this to happen soon.'

'We have your details,' Martin said, 'and will be in touch.'

Martin leaned across to the door and opened it for Steven. Steven hesitated a moment, as though something else was on his mind. Whatever it was, he swallowed it down and stepped from the room. Martin waited for his new client to get a few steps away and then quietly closed the door before returning back to his table.

*

True to his word, Martin had received the government's answer to Steven's contract request within a few days. An affirmative. On the very same day, Marin had also set about planning how they would take care of Nate.

The plan was simple: Interview him, just as they interviewed all the other troubled *bad-influences,* and then toss him off a hotel balcony. After, obviously, plying him with enough alcohol that it would show in the autopsy reports that he was *well* over the legal limit. Some people would question whether his death was suicide, others would question whether it was an accident brought about by being drunk and out of control and yet all would put the blame on him. The fact he was so out of his head, at the time of death, coupled with the negative interview they'd run just before his untimely death - it would all paint a poor picture of him. This wasn't a man to look up to. This wasn't someone to aspire to be. If anything, he would be a cautionary tale as to why you *shouldn't* drink.

'Okay that all sounds fine,' Steven said during the phone call with Martin. 'And when will this happen?'

'You tell us. Our partner magazine would like to schedule and interview with your client,' Martin said. 'Is there a time that would be convenient?'

'He'll bitch about it no doubt but he has a small show this coming weekend, ahead of the main tour... Could see you after that? Probably be the best time, to be fair, given his mood when he usually comes off stage.'

Martin smiled. 'Sounds perfect. I shall transfer you to my secretary who can take all the finer details from you. How's that sound?'

Steven paused a moment. 'I mean it sounds great but...'

'But?'

'Nothing bad. I just can't believe how fast this is moving.'

'You did advise us time was of the essence.'

'No, no. And it is. I just... No. This is all good.' Steve added, 'I'm just impressed.'

'Well, we like to provide a thorough and most excellent service.' When Steven failed to say anything else, Martin added, 'I'll pass you over to my secretary and - once again - on behalf of myself and the company, thank you for choosing us to help take out your trash…'

Part Eight

It's Just Business

'So why the change of plan? If everything was okay, like you said it was, why are we doing this now?' Carolyne asked, impatient to know the reasons behind the change. She pushed, 'Did he change his mind? But then, if he did, why are we even torturing this guy? Surely we should just be letting him go or just terminating him anyway given that he can identify us...'

'You.'

'I'm sorry?'

'Given that he can identify you. Unless, of course, you're saying that if we did let him go and he did go to the authorities - you would point the finger to all of us too?'

'Don't twist what I mean. I'm not in the mood for playing games and...'

'And I'm not in the mood for your tone. Now if you'd let me finish... Everything was fine but then our client got cold feet in the *way* we were going to dispose of Mr. Nasty. If we kill him off in a way which leaves a bitter aftertaste with his followers then they will just want a refund on the concert tickets. They won't want the special, limited edition ticket Mr. Gibson has in mind. Furthermore, album sales will not pick up as he initially hoped…'

'When have we ever done this for the money?'

'In this instance we are doing it for the money of our client and had we not been happy with such an agreement, we wouldn't have gone ahead with it. The decision was made and that's not for you or I to argue. Now, he went away knowing what we were going to do and - not so long ago - Mr. Gibson phoned me to explain his concerns. Furthermore he offered more money if we changed our plans to make things easier for him. In this instance, he wishes for a tape to be leaked showing the torture, and murder, of Mr. Nasty…'

'So it's just about the money now?'

Martin laughed. 'It's always just about the money. It's just, this time, it's more obvious than the other occasions.'

'I thought it was more about taking the trash from society and the money was secondary.'

'When they're big influencers then yes, you're right. In the case of Mr. Nasty though... Really, what is his reach? A few thousand? A few hundred thousand? He's hardly in the same league as everyone else - which you yourself have said to me before, did you not?'

'I did.'

'So - in this case it's more about the money and we're still getting rid of someone who is - to be honest - a black stain in the population.' Martin continued, 'I ask again, do you want me to pull you out of there or do you want to go ahead and see this through?' Martin laughed. 'I assure you, we have some very special treats lined up for Mr. Nasty and - so long as your stomach is strong - you'll have a particularly interesting time. Not forgetting, of course, that you'll also get the monies owed to you.' He paused and then asked, 'So what is it to be?'

*

Carolyne walked back into the room. She noticed the camera was recording now and so quietly closed the door behind her as best she could, seeing that it was covered in plastic. Once in, she returned to where she'd initially been standing against the wall.

Mr. White smiled to her beneath his surgical mask. 'Good to have you back with us. We were just about to start and were wondering as to whether you'd be joining us.'

'I'm sorry,' she said, 'I wasn't feeling very well.'

Carolyne knew her place. She was an interviewer and whilst she helped move things forward, she was not in the same pay grade as these individuals; the ones who took charge of the contract's final moments. She also knew that, despite the smiles and their polite ways, these were not the nice people they pretended to be.

'I'm terribly sorry to hear that. If you need us to wait a little longer, so you can compose yourself, we would be more than happy to do so for you.' Mr. White turned to Nate and said, 'You won't mind giving her an extra few minutes, would you?'

His response came in a gurgled mess of strange sounds and dribble as Nate struggled against the restraints binding him in place.

'I'll be fine,' Carolyne said, already embarrassed that such a fuss was being made of her.

Mr. White paused a moment, his eyes locked to her, and then - content she was ready, as stated - he nodded.

'Okay then,' he said, 'let's turn this up to eleven.' He turned to Nate. 'Spinal Tap quote for you. How'd you like that?' He didn't wait for an answer. He turned to one of the three other masked men and said, 'Pass me the corkscrew and let us get this show on the road.'

In a panic, Nate squirmed against the restraints despite knowing they weren't going to give and, even if they did, he had nowhere to run. Through the ball-gag, he tried once again to scream out.

'Oh, please, Mr. Nasty... They'll be none of that noise. At least not yet. Not before we've actually begun.' An unseen smile from behind the mask as he took a silver corkscrew from one of the other masked men. 'Thank you. Very kind of you.' Mr. White leaned over where Nate lay so that he could look him direct in the eyes. Not that it brought much reassurance to Nate, he calmly informed him, 'I just want you to know that this isn't personal. Now I cannot speak on behalf of the rest of the crew, or even the young lady here but - from my point of view - I wish you no malice nor harm. Unfortunately, with that being said, it is all down to business.' He shrugged causing the corkscrew to shine as it caught the light of the overhead light. 'What can you do, hey? Bills to pay.' He held up the corkscrew so that Nate could get a really good look at it. 'Now do you know what this is?' He laughed. 'Of course you do. It's a corkscrew. I am sure you have used many in your life, what with your enjoyment of alcohol. Well, we won't be opening bottles with *this* one you'll most likely be displeased to hear.'

Without hesitation, Mr. White set the sharp pointed end of the corkscrew against Nate's cheek and dragged upwards. The motion, and weight pressed upon it, was enough to rip into Nate's skin and make him scream in pain through the plastic gag. His cries didn't stop Mr. White there though as he proceeded to pull the corkscrew back down Nate's face so that the cut went up and then back down in a straight line close to the initial slice. It wasn't enough to cause blood to free-flow but it was enough to make it look as though some kind of cat, or something similar, had attacked him.

'Screaming already?' Mr. White almost sounded disappointed. 'Really? This is superficial. This will heal in time and I doubt there will be anything left to show for what you just went through. If you think about it, you got off quite lightly compared to Mr. Watts; that man you attacked in the bar. Of course we tried to track him down to speak to him, in order to find out the lasting damage your vicious attack but - well - we were called in last minute for this and he's somewhat hard to track down.' Mr. White teased, 'We could have asked you for his contact details but we figured you probably didn't exchange them before you disfigured him for life.'

Nate tried to speak but to no avail. Instead of words, just more saliva dribbled from the side of his mouth.

'Look at you,' Mr. White continued to tease, 'look like a retard, all this dribble. And to think, going from other stories about yourself, you always seemed so keen on everyone else swallowing but of course, those rules don't apply to you.' Mr. White shook his head solemnly and then continued to scratch up Nate's face with the corkscrew. 'Because we can't find him and haven't have enough time to really look into what happened to Dean Watts, it's fair to say we are going to have to do a little guesswork. Now I won't lie, it is hard to say whether you're going to get off lighter than you really deserve or whether you're going to come off worse but - well... That's the way it goes.'

Mr. White scratched Nate's face again as Nate continued to thrash around in an attempt to pull away from the corkscrew. In truth, he only made it worse for himself.

'You might want to try and lie still, Mr. Nasty. We don't want to actually blind you now, do we? Although - maybe that's what happened to Mr. Watts? You put the glass in his face. Maybe you blinded him?' He stood up straight for a moment, clicking his back in the process. 'Which means - tit for tat - we really should take at least one of your eyes. What do you say?'

'Mmmmmmnnnngghhhhhhhhh.....'

'I'm terribly sorry, good sir, but I don't speak gibberish. I shall simply have to imagine you said something along the lines of, yes, you agree in that we should take one of your eyes. Well, given how you potentially blinded that poor fan in the bar, I think that is very fair of you to be so agreeable.'

Mr. White nodded to two of his colleagues. As though going through a well practised routine, they stepped forward and both held Nate's head in position to stop him from moving away, or attempting to. With Nate's head firmly being held, Mr. White lined up the corkscrew.

Part Nine

Eye For An Eye

The camera is lifted from the tripod which causes the screen to flicker for just a split second. There is a mechanical whirring noise as the picture zooms in closer to Nate's face until his eye fills the screen. It's brown. It's watery. Tears of fear? With the camera so zoomed in, there is a little shake to the picture thanks to the camera operator's unsteady hand.

Nate is making noise but that's all it is: Noise.

Two of the torturers hold his head in place with visible force but - from this angle - they're mostly out of shot.

The corkscrew comes down into shot. The metal shines brilliantly in the light and looks truly stunning in this 4K definition.

Nate closes his eye as the corkscrew nears. Mr. White doesn't need the eye to be open. If anything, Nate has made it worse for himself.

The pointed tip of the corkscrew presses against the now-closed eyelid. At this point it is not hard enough to pierce the skin. It is enough to push the eyelid in slightly though and - if the corkscrew were to be pulled away - leave a little indentation behind.

Nate's noise sounds more panicked now; picked up by the so-so microphone attached to the camera. The microphone isn't good enough to pick up what Mr. White is saying at this particular moment, thanks to the pitiful cries Nate makes.

[VOLUME UP]

Barely audible:

'… you slashed at his face with the broken glass you probably robbed him of his sight fairly quickly. Hours of surgery at the hospital, wasted in trying to save it…'

The camera zooms in further, accompanied by that same whirring noise as before. Only the eyelid and tip of the corkscrew are in shot now. The camera shakes increase.

'… This might seem like it's slow but - in truth - it's probably quicker than all he went through with his eye trauma so, you should count yourself lucky.'

The corkscrew pushes in and, at the same time, twists.

Nate screams through the pain as the point easily pierces through his eyelid with just a little more pressure. As the corkscrew continues to twist, the flesh of the ripped eyelid starts to wrap itself around it.

Nate's scream changes pitch and goes higher still.

[VOLUME DOWN]

As the corkscrew twirls deeper into the hidden eyeball, more of the eyelid rips away and wraps itself around the corkscrew. A clear liquid seeps out from between ripped flesh and the metal instrument. It runs down Nate's cheek like a tear as Nate's scream continues to change pitch.

The corkscrew stops. Now it is only moving thanks to Nate's own (slight) movements. His cries do not stop though as he struggles to keep conscious, not that it would have upset him to pass out if he'd stopped to really think about it.

A mechanical whir as the camera slowly zooms out.

The corkscrew starts to twist again, the opposite way this time as it is slowly pulled from the mangled mess of ripped flesh and ruptured eyeball. As it comes out, there is a small trickle of blood from the torn flesh. This blood mixes with the cloudy-white juice from inside the eyeball *resembling a look not dissimilar to raspberry ripple ice-cream.*

Nate is silent now. The pain and experience all being too much for him. He has passed out.

Not picked up by the camera is a scent reminiscent of the stink lingering outside a butcher's shop on a warm summer's day.

The camera moves closer to Nate's face so that, even on a low volume, the microphone picks up the sounds of squelching as the corkscrew continues to be removed from the destroyed socket. Close your eyes and without the picture playing on the screen, you'd easily be able to imagine three fingers fucking in and out of a moist pussy on the verge of gushing a fountain of cum.

The end of the corkscrew pulls free. Disappointingly, for the viewers at home, there is no eyeball impaled on the end of it. There are only tatters of flesh, wet with blood and God only knows what else which makes up the insides of a - now - burst eye.

[STATIC]

Part Ten

It's Not Torture If They're Unconscious

Mr. White tossed the corkscrew to one of his accomplices more or less the moment he'd pulled it from Nate's socket. His accomplice caught it and set it down on the floor, out of the way, before he asked, 'What would you like next?'

'Nothing yet. Little point in continuing if he is unconscious.' He turned to the camera operator and instructed him, 'Turn the camera off. Save the battery.'

As per his demand, the camera was switched off.

'Why not just kill him now?' Carolyne asked.

Mr. White slowly turned to her. There was a way in which he moved which was just downright creepy. Slow. Menacing. Almost hunched over with his hands held close to his chest. He paused a moment with his eyes fixed on Carolyne.

'I'm sorry? Did you say something?'

She knew she had overstepped the mark but Nate had been tortured as per the requests of the management. As far as she was concerned, the job was complete. Why waste time in torturing him further when they could just kill him now and be done with it. Get the mess cleaned up, get out, release the interview and get the tape to the media soon after. They'd done all that had been requested!

Carolyne said, 'We were asked to torture him. He has been tortured. You got it on

tape, and I was looking at the camera as it was being filmed and it looks suitably disgusting so - well done.' She added. 'We've done all that was asked. Let's finish up, collect the pay cheque and get home to our families…'

Mr. White slowly shook his head from side to side. 'We took an eye from him and he passed out. This isn't a man who has been tortured. This is a man who has had his eye removed. To torture someone is to put them through hell, not show them the door to it and then pull back.' He addressed his crew. 'Use the salts and wake him up. Administer some pain relief if necessary. What we have next is more physical pain than mental so - as long as we ensure his immediate pain is managed - he should be able to cope quite easily with what is next.' He laughed. 'Well, on a pain level. Mentally it's a different story but...' He turned back to Carolyne and said, 'Torture doesn't just have to be about pain inflicted, does it? Mental games are just as important.'

Carolyne didn't argue as - behind Mr. White - the team started to use smelling salts to bring Nate back around. The moment he did, he started to scream (as best he could) with the pain of his eye. Carolyne watched as a needle was jabbed into his arm. The clear liquid within it was introduced to his blood stream.

Nate's moans were fairly quick to quieten down as the fast-acting medicine gave some much needed, but not necessarily deserved, relief.

Mr. White took his position next to where Nate lay once more and looked down at him with false pity in his eyes.

'How was your sleep? Did you dream nice things? A happy little interval before we continue with our little home video?' He looked up to the man who'd originally been operating the camera and gave him a nod. The man set the camera back on the tripod and powered it up.

The camera's battery whirred to life.

Mr. White glanced over to another of his three colleagues and said, 'I do believe it's dinner time.' He looked at Carolyne. Behind his mask, he was smiling. As a woman, he figured she would probably appreciate this one more than the eye. Even if she hadn't been put through it herself at any point, she would be grateful on behalf of all women-kind who *had* been put through what was to follow.

Mr. White teased, 'You're going to like this.' He looked back to Nate and continued the tease, 'You… Well, I don't know you. You *might* actually enjoy this which is why we had to change it up a little. You know… Just in case your impending meal was, secretly, to your taste. After all - this isn't supposed to be a treat now, is it?'

Groggy but awake, Nate tried to speak around the uncomfortable lump of the plastic ball in his mouth. Unsurprisingly, his words weren't understood. Mr. White immediately slapped him hard on his chest.

'No!' Mr. White explained, 'You don't get to talk. And I am glad you brought this up now because we do have to remove the gag from your mouth. But, when we do, you're not to say anything. You're not to plead, you're not to argue, you're not to say a single word. Do you understand me?' He continued, 'If I hear anything other than the occasional whimper, moan or even a scream… If I hear *anything*… I swear, my team and I will remove your other eye. Now - as it stands - we are being generous in letting you keep that so do not test us. I can assure you that you will lose. And, if we go down that route and end up taking your second eye… If you still try and talk to us… We will remove your tongue. Who knows though - maybe we will use that as some dressing for your eye-wound if we do? Roll it up nice and tight and stick it in your empty socket.' Mr. White cracked his knuckles. He finished with, 'We can do things that you have never even thought about before, let alone believed possible once they'd been explained to you. So, when I remove your gag, please do keep that in mind.'

Mr. White lifted Nate's head from the table and pulled the gag free. It was obvious from the expression on his face, even with his eye missing, that Nate was desperate to say something so Mr. White reminded him, 'Not a word. Not a single word.' He added, 'And if you are good and play nice, I am sure we might let you have your say towards the end.' He looked over to Carolyne and said, 'But that will be up to my colleague over there. I'm just here for the torture.'

Behind his protective glasses, he winked to Carolyne. He spoke of being there just for one thing but Carolyne was under no illusion that all the time he was present, Mr. White was very much the one in charge.

One of Mr. White's accomplices presented a lidded plastic beaker to Mr. White. Before he took hold of it, Mr. White pulled some rubber gloves from his pocket and proceeded to put them on. After all, he knew what was in the beaker. There was no way he wanted that shit on his hands.

'A delectable treat for you, we have, right here.' Mr. White explained. 'Now before I show you what it is, I want you to truly appreciate the effort we went to in order to get this for you. Without knowing the effort, I fear you wouldn't be as appreciative about it and - well - our team would most likely find that to be somewhat upsetting. So… Let me tell you a little story.'

The camera was focused on Nate's face for the duration of what Mr. White would have to say.

Part Eleven
None Will Be Wasted

Mr. White narrated. Nate's tired mind filled in the blanks, not that he really wanted them filled.

'Both men and women were hired through various adult magazines, websites and such like. They were brought in for an interview for a fabricated job. Once sitting with our team, they were informed what was really required. They would each be needed to suck off a grown man. Given that the applicants were there believing they were to appear in an actual film, this wasn't a big ask of them.'

The white, clinical-looking room was empty other than a number of pillows situated in a long line along the floor. As the groups filed in, the men (whom were to be sucked to completion) stood on the right and the "suckers" stood on the left. Like a Mexican Wave, the "suckers" dropped to their knees and onto the pillows. Men and women, all of legal age, ready and willing to suck on the hard cocks, both cut and uncut, now just inches from their faces.

'They were all paid. The men getting sucked and the men and women doing the sucking. Equal rate for all.'

A voice came through an internal speaker informing everyone that they could begin. Without further instruction, cocks were taken in mouths and heads started bobbing up and down on shafts of various sizes. Slurping and sucking noises, wet and dribbly as some of the workers just teased the head as others swallowed the whole erection down the back of their throats. Some worked fast. Some worked slow and teased the men standing before them. Some used their hands on the shaft, stroking up and down after various speeds. Others gave their hands a little twist with a strong wrist. Some tickled balls, some gripped the man's buttocks and pulled them closer as though to get more of the cock in their mouth. Some even teased the arsehole of the man they sucked; circling it with a finger as others dared push deeper.

'The rules were simple in that they had to take the ejaculate in their mouth. Once they took the pay load, they could do as they pleased with regards to what happened next but they *had* to take it in their mouths. Some wanted to swallow, some wanted to spit. Those who chose to spit it back out were asked to ensure they got it into a beaker we provided them with before they went in.'

Some of the men came quickly thanks to the technique of the person they were partnered with. Their partners looked up at them with satisfaction on their faces; happy they were able to get them over the edge in double quick time. Some spat directly into the beaker, some let the warm cum spill over their bottom lip, thick and creamy, and run down their chin where they proceeded to collect it up into the beaker. Others - fully intending to spit the salty goo - were so taken off guard by the suddenness of the ejaculation that they accidentally swallowed it down in a heavy gulp which was accompanied by a shudder as they felt the semen dribble down into their gut like a warm liquor.

'Those who swallowed, of which there were a fair few to be fair, were given the promise of more money if they were happy to undertake a small procedure immediately after they left the room.'

The "swallowers" were laid upon a table. They were unconscious, ready for an operation they'd signed off on in exchange for treble the initial rate offered. A small tube would be inserted down their throat and into their oesophagus. On the end of the tube, there was a small spoon shaped device which was used to remove a sample of the recently gulped spunk, and anything else it happened to collect on the way as it scraped the person's insides. This was then removed and added to a larger beaker where the other sperm donations had been poured.

'What we didn't tell those employed to do the sucking was that we had different sorts of people lined up for them. I don't mean different backgrounds; religious and where they were born and all that. I mean different states of health. Some had mild sexually transmitted diseases. Some had more *serious* conditions. We collected healthy samples, unhealthy, *really* unhealthy… We collected it all.'

A man in the final days of living with AIDS lies in a hospital bed on a ventilator as a rubber-gloved nurse strokes his cock hard and fast with both hands. Next to her, there is a beaker ready for the deposit.

'Wonder why we collected it all?'

*

Mr. White opened the beaker up and looked into it with obvious disgust on his face, despite his expression mostly being hidden by the surgical mask.

'Your groupies. How many of them gave you head? How many of them wanted to stop at the point of taking your dirty load in their mouth? Not very nice of you then when you boast about how you forced them to not only take the load but to swallow it too. Well - just as you now know how it feels to lose an eye, like you did with that poor gentleman who approached you in the bar… Well, now you're going to learn what it is like to take a shot against your will.' Mr. White smiled behind his mask. 'You know what I'm going to do with this beaker and the contents, right?'

'Please…'

'Ah ah ah… Remember what I said? Want to lose your other eye? Because you will. And, furthermore, you will still have to drink this down. All of it. And, just like those you forced before you, you have to swallow it all down. Take your medicine like a man.'

Mr. White dipped his fingers into the pot and scooped some of the mixture up. It wasn't as sperm-like as you'd imagine thanks to the specimens collected from within the swallowers. It was creamy white tinged with a yellow and pink not normal for such a load. A congealed gravy mixture; how it tends to go when left on the side for too long before being disposed of, with a thick "skin" on the top of the slick.

'I'm glad I have a mask covering my nose and mouth,' Mr. White said, 'because - I can only imagine what this reeks of.'

He held it under Nate's nose. Nate tried to turn away from it so Mr. White nodded to his colleagues. Once again they grabbed Nate's head and held it firmly in place. Again, Mr. White held his fingers under Nate's nose. A dollop of the mixture stretched down and touched upon Nate's top lip. He retched in response.

Fish. Sweat. Cheese. Ham?

'Now we went to a lot of expense to get this. Especially at such short notice. So, you're going to be grateful when you swallow this entire mixture down. I'm going to let you even talk once you do. Not before. After. You get to say, thank you Mr. White, thank you.'

Nate tried to shake his head but was unable to thanks to being held firmly in place. Mr. White put the beaker against Nate's bottom lip and started to tilt it. In response, Nate clamped his mouth shut tight.

Mr. White laughed. Did he really think he was going to get away with not eating the gunk?

'Heard the expression, rubbing salt into the wound?'

Mr. White put his dirtied fingers into Nate's open socket and rimmed around the edges. Nate, in turn, screamed as the salt mixed with the open flesh wound and, as he did so, Mr. White tipped the mixture.

Part Twelve
All The Flavours

Nate gagged as the *cold custard* trickled into his mouth in unhealthy lumps of a snot-like ooze. As the repulsive taste - heavy in salt - hit, he rolled his tongue to the side of his mouth in an effort to get it out of the way of the unwanted flavour. He coughed and a spittle of spunk fired from his mouth only to land on the side of his face. It was so thick in texture it didn't snake down his cheek like a tear, it simply stuck in place where it proceeded to dry.

Sensing the vomit coming, Mr. White tipped as much of the remainder in as he dared before he quickly dropped the beaker to the floor.

With the others holding Nate in place, Mr. White clamped his mouth shut by pushing up hard under his chin. Only when Nate started bubbling the spunk cocktail out from between his parted lips did Mr. White then put his second hand over Nate's mouth forcing the mess to not spill out any further.

'Swallow it. Just like you made them swallow it. You swallow it all.'

Beneath the three men holding him down, Nate struggled and writhed around but to no avail. He gagged and choked on the mess, desperate not to take it further but - slowly - with little gulps, it slipped down his gullet; an unpleasant tasting concoction similar to forcing down the more tar-like of cough syrups.

Only when Mr. White thought the majority of it was digested did he pull away, removing his hands from Nate. With a nod to his colleagues, they too backed away and - the moment they did - Nate turned his head to the side and violently vomited. It didn't taste good going down and it didn't taste any better coming back up; bitter and chunkier with strings of what looked like partially digested carrot.

Nate still gagged as the fresh taste of semen-specimens lingered in his mouth, along with the more recent acidic flavouring of his own sick. Feeling traumatised, a tear rolled from his eye. Unlike the earlier dollop of spunk, this didn't stick. It trickled down his cheek but got him no sympathy from his tormentors.

'You can stop that for a minute,' Mr. White said to the man working the camera. 'There's still much to film and we don't want to waste tape.'

The camera stopped recording just as Nate vomited for a second time.

Mr. White continued, 'Let him get the sick out of his system. We don't want the viewers at home switching off so soon because they don't have a stomach for it.' He leaned down to Nate but at a safe distance in case he vomited again. He asked, 'Did you want a glass of water? I'm sure we could get you a nice glass of water?'

Nate sicked up for a third time. This time, mixed into the bile, was much of the previously swallowed juices.

'Okay, can we get him some water please?'

One of the mask men walked from the room. He was gone less than a few seconds when he came in with a paper cup from a well known fast food chain. The cup was covered with a plastic lid and, from that, a straw poked through. Dutifully, the man held the cup out to Mr. White who took it from him.

'Sorry for the backwash. We don't actually have drinks just lying around for you because, well, this isn't a holiday. But I feel a little bad for what you've just been put through so, yes, we have this. It's nothing bad, just one of the drinks left over from our lunch so, here you go…'

Mr. White held the drink closer to Nate's mouth and nodded to the camera-man who hit record. Nate hesitated.

'I won't offer it again. If you don't want it, it's no skin off my nose, I'm just being friendly.'

He went to move the cup away but, as he did so, Nate lifted his head slightly in an effort to reach the straw. Mr. White smiled.

Nate drew in through the straw and immediately sprayed the fluid back out again in a fine mist through pursed lips, causing those around (who *knew*) to laugh. Carolyne didn't laugh. Mr. White noticed her lack of reaction so took it upon himself to explain.

'You don't know this story?'

*

(BEFORE)

With too much alcohol for her body to cope with, Sharon couldn't help but to pass out in a crumpled heap on the hotel suite's sofa. She'd flaked out pretty much at the start of the evening; a mess of a whore who clearly couldn't handle her booze much to the amusement of the band members.

When Steven had failed to wake the girl at the end of the party, desperate to clear the suite out of unwanted guests, Nate had stepped forward with an idea.

'She just needs a little water splashed on her face.'

To a normal person, it made sense. Steven figured they'd get some water from the ensuite bathroom and throw it on her. The sudden shock would be enough to pull the unconscious slut from her sleep and then, she'd be pushed out into the streets. It was certainly better than having to call 999, worrying about whether she'd given herself alcohol poisoning...

The problem was, Nate wasn't a normal person and before Steven had a chance to admit to it being a good idea, Nate had already pulled his soft dick from the front of his leather pants.

'Just needs a little water,' he said. With that he relaxed and as he did so, he started to urinate over the woman's face. 'Come on, lads.'

Nate's band members, Joe and Sid, jumped up from where they'd crashed down. Laughing, they drunkenly stumbled over to where Nate continued to relieve himself on the bitch. They didn't need to be asked twice and soon each had their cock in their hand too. Stood in a line, together like the Three Musketeers with swords in hands, they followed Nate's lead.

Steven watched on disgusted, but not wanting to say anything for fear of upsetting "the stars", as all three pissed on the woman. Slowly, she started to come round and the moment she opened her eyes - the panic and disgust hit home hard. Her reaction just made the guys laugh more. Sharon got the last laugh when she made money from the press, selling her story.

Nate laughed, 'All the flavours!'

*

Carolyne hated what she'd heard of Nate and knew he deserved all he was getting now but, even so, she didn't like it. Whilst the others laughed at Nate, who was still coughing and spluttering after his refreshing mouthful of piss, she still couldn't see a reason to laugh. He'd had an eye removed, been forced to eat the cum and now a mouth of piss and yet she knew, these guys would still have many, many more tricks up their sleeves to hurt him with - both mentally and physically. Enough was enough though, surely? They had all they needed for the tape.

'We probably have enough now,' Carolyne said, referring to the footage.

Mr. White shook his head. 'No. We are providing a service and - when we do - we always go over and above.' He suggested, 'Maybe you'd enjoy it more if you were to join in with us instead of standing over there, up against the wall like a scared little kitten?'

Carolyne bit her tongue despite the temptation to tell him to go and fuck himself. That wasn't out of respect though. She genuinely worried that, if she pushed his buttons in such a way, he might turn on her in the same way he worked on Nate.

'I'm fine where I am, thank you.'

'But - I don't know - maybe you think we are being too cruel to our friend here? Maybe you're warming to him and, actually, you think we should let him go? Is that what's going on?'

'It's not,' Carolyne said.

Mr. White turned his attention back to Nate. He asked him, 'What about you? Do you think we should let you go? Do you think you have learned your lesson and will be nicer to people now? Or do you even see these as lessons? Maybe you think we're just doing this for the fun of it? I mean you know about the eye. You know why we took that, right? For what you did to that man in the bar. And forcing you to eat the cum? I think we were pretty clear as to why we did that too. But the piss? Maybe you have forgotten about that woman? The one in the hotel? The one whose face you all pissed on? She's the reason I gave you a mouthful of urine... It wasn't because I thought it was a good idea. Oh but look too...' Mr. White took the lid off the plastic cup and look into the urine contained within. 'Look at this… Stored at room temperature… Cloudy, dark yellow… Even through my mask I can smell it… It's gross, right? Sugar puffs? Guess they eat asparagus although I'm not sure where the guy would have got asparagus from. Oh yeah, that's right… It's a man's piss you just chugged down. Some homeless guy who was only too thrilled to take a little cash in exchange for a cup of his waste.' Mr. White shuddered. 'Can only imagine the taste.' Mr. White shook his head. 'Sorry I went off on a tangent. We were asking whether you wanted us to let you go?'

'I'm not who…'

Mr. White put his finger up against Nate's mouth, shushing him quiet in the process. 'It is a simple yes and no answer. I don't want anything more out of you than a yes or a no. So - let us try again. Do you want us to let you go?'

Mr. White removed his finger away from Nate's mouth.

'Yes.'

Mr. White nodded. 'I thought that might be your answer but there is one thing from your life stories which really troubles me and we're going to need to deal with that before we go any further.' He paused a moment and added, 'Yes or no answer. Do you know what that story might be?'

Nate shook his head. 'No.'

'Well that is disappointing. Either you've done so much bad stuff that you can't decide which is the worst or you don't think what you've done is bad. I'll be honest with you, Mr. Nasty, I'm not sure which answer out of those two I would prefer to hear from you.'

Nate didn't say anything.

Part Thirteen

The Statement

The screams turned him on more. I begged for him to get off. He told me what he planned to do and laughed. I said no. I told him I didn't want it. I didn't want him. He slapped me with the open palm of his hand. It stung and I felt my eyes well up. He asked if I was going to cry and I told him to fuck off. He laughed and asked me again; was I going to cry? I told him no. I wouldn't give him the satisfaction of seeing my tears. He seemed mad and hit me again. Open palmed. It stung. After the second slap, he asked me again whether I was going to cry and, again, I said I wouldn't. A tear spilled from my eye when he hit me for the third time and - when it did - he smiled. Next thing, as I struggled beneath him, he leaned down and licked the tear away. He told me he liked the taste. He said it was salty. I had given him something salty and, in return, he would give me something salty. I screamed again for him to get off but he refused. Instead he asked me where I wanted his salty load. Did I want it on my face? Did I want it on my tits? In my pussy? In my ass? I told him again that I didn't want it but before I got the sentence out, I felt his hands around my throat. He was grinning, looking down at me... His grip was tight and I was struggling to get the necessary air in but he didn't care. If anything, he seemed to like it going by what I could feel pressing up against me through his shorts.

I didn't want to cry. I didn't want him having the satisfaction of thinking he was hurting me, given how he was getting off on it. I'd lost count of the number of times I had said no to him. I had wanted to meet him. Ever since the first album, I had wanted to hear him but - I didn't want this. I wanted a signature on a vinyl I had. This was all him. A fee, he said, for the cost of his signature.

Had his hands not been stopping the air, I would have gasped in pain - maybe even screamed - when I felt his prick enter me. I was so scared. I was so dry. The initial penetration ripped me internally; a short, sharp sting which made me wince. It didn't get any better when he started to fuck me harder and faster - going as deep as he could. He's not a small man and every time he thrust in, it felt as though I was being impaled. Whenever his hands moved from my neck, I screamed for him to get off. I begged for him to stop but - he didn't care. He was just telling me that he knew I wanted it. He said I wanted it from the moment I saw him but that wasn't true! I'm not that sort of person! I had a boyfriend! I had a partner and I was happy and he took all that from me, and more...

When he came, he breathed hard in my face. I could smell his halitosis and I gagged. He repulsed me. I liked his music but he has always repulsed me as a person and here he was, on top of me. Worse. When he pulled out, I could still feel where he had been and I could feel his semen and...

My partner left me because I couldn't stand his touch anymore. He blamed me for what had happened too. He said I had encouraged it and I wanted it but that wasn't the case. I swear that wasn't the case. I just wanted his signature and... My partner left me and I have nightmares. I have bad dreams where I re-live the moment over and over again. I get to feel him rip me. I get to feel his hands on me and around my throat. I get to smell that stink of rotten teeth and bad gums. Hear that sigh at the point of ejaculation. I can still feel him between my legs and his mess spilling out of me. I can see feel that fear, wondering what was going to happen to me when he finally did get off - leaving me on the floor where he'd first pushed me. I wasn't sure if he was going to kill me. I wasn't sure if he was going to threaten me into silence, try and buy it or what...

It took me so long to step forward because I was scared. I was scared of him, I was scared of his band members. I was scared of all of them. The only reason I finally came forward is because I started thinking about other people in my position; fans who found themselves an opportunity to meet him. People he could take advantage of because of who he is. And it made me sick. It made me physically sick to think of him out and about, forcing himself on these other women as though it is his right. He doesn't deserve fans. He doesn't deserve people thinking he is the best. He doesn't deserve the truth of who he is to be hidden away.

He deserves prison.

*

'Yet you never got prison, did you?' Mr. White sighed. 'The girl, only seventeen years old, was made out to be a liar as - from out of nowhere - you had an alibi which got you off the hook entirely. But then, it's a hard crime to nail down when there's no DNA evidence and no one saw anything… It's made harder when you're able to provide someone willing to be a back up to whatever lie you said to get off the hook.'

'But…'

'Did you like your tongue? I will cut it from your mouth to save hearing excuses or lies, you hear me? We both know you raped that woman whether you were cleared from the court case or not. We both know the type of *man* that you are. You know, when I learned more about you and got to know who you *really* were… I would have taken this job for free. You think you're better than everyone else because you write songs and shout them through a microphone. You think you're something special but you're not. I once said that we are all equal. Humans, that is. Yes, some may have more luck in life than others and put themselves in a better position but we are all still human. That's it. But you believe yourself to be some kind of God among men. You treat people as though they are under you and you get a kick out of it. You're a piece of shit. Like the song "Genital Mutilation" and the banned video. A video which became infamous despite hardly everyone ever seeing it…' Mr. White continued, 'I haven't seen it. My colleagues haven't seen it.' He looked at Carolyne. 'Have you?'

She shook her head.

Mr. White said, 'Yet we have *heard* about it because of how outrageous it is. A song talking about forced female cutting - seemingly against it and yet a video in which you...' Mr. White shook his head. He asked again, 'Did you want to survive this day? That, again, is a yes or no answer.'

'Yes.'

'Then you must know where we are going with this.'

Part Fourteen
Forced Female Cutting

Bored with taking pot shots at their own government, *The Black Room Manuscripts* had decided to take a shot at governments across the world who wouldn't ban the act of forced female cutting. Not only did it give them the chance to scream obscene lyrics down the microphone, about "cut cunts" but it made them seem relevant in a time when social media platforms were all highlighting the controversial topic. And, whilst obscene, that would have been fine had they left it there but then there was *that* video.

The concert's location was never disclosed. It was simply stated that, during a performance of the song, female members of the crowd were invited up to the stage to take part in a stunt. They were only told what they had to do once they were on stage and the rest of the audience was loudly cheering them on, making it hard for them to back down without looking like they were scared.

The women stripped off their bottoms and laid upon the stage with their undercarriage exposed to the cheering audience as a stage-hand gave them a piece of thick card each. The aim of the game was simple: Whilst Nate sang the lyrics of the three minute twenty song, the women had to run the edge of the card across their pussies. The one who managed to cut themselves the most won the game; if winning was such a thing in this instance. At the end of the song, Nate sang about tears of the world falling for the victims of such an atrocity in an over-the-top, pretentious piece of verse reminiscent to any part of Michael Jackson's *Earth Song*. It was out of character for a band which tended to scream more than sing but, whilst their style might have changed for that particular moment, their destructive attitudes hadn't. The moment "tears" were sung about, the cutting ladies were doused with water pistols filled with vinegar. Their screams were a part of punk history, urban legend and - the chorus.

Soon everyone was talking about the video of the event, and it was soon reported to have been banned by all channels. When people heard about it being online somewhere, they'd race to where it was and hit the download button unaware that, they'd just given their system AIDS. It didn't stop people from talking about the video though and whenever they did, it was always the same story: A friend of a friend of a friend had seen it and described it to them and - by all accounts - it was fucking brutal.

*

Mr. White leaned closer to Nate and whispered, 'I want you to cut yourself like you made those girls cut themselves.' He added, 'Like I said - I would have taken this job for nothing so the fact I'm even saying you can go home if you do this, that's something you shouldn't take lightly.'

A tear rolled from Nate's good eye. He hesitated a moment and then said, 'Permission to speak?'

Impressed with his sudden manners, Mr. White couldn't help but to smile from behind his mask. 'Certainly.'

'You need to call my manager.'

'I do?'

'They'll pay you whatever you want if you just let me go. I won't say a word. I'll say I didn't see your faces. I'll say I don't remember who took me.' He looked to Carolyne and said, 'I'll say you never showed up for the interview... Please, I just want to go home.'

Mr. White laughed. 'You sound completely different here, begging like a coward. Where's this infamous front man I'd heard so much about? Where's this mouthy gob-shite of an individual?'

'Please if you call them...'

'To be fair...' He paused a moment and then glanced over to Carolyne. 'Can I tell him?'

She shrugged.

Mr. White continued, 'I can tell him.' He looked back down to Nate and continued, 'Steven Gibson is waiting for our phone call as it happens. But he isn't waiting for a ransom. He is waiting for confirmation that it is done.'

Mr. White's accomplice spoke up, 'Should I turn the camera off?'

Mr. White shook his head. 'We can edit this out. It's fine.' He continued, 'That manager you think will help you out of this, he's waiting for the call to say you're dead. Why? Because he is the one who ordered this to be done. Your album sales aren't doing great, your concerts aren't doing brilliantly. You are worth more to him dead than you're worth alive. So, yes, a Mr. Steven Gibson ordered us to take you down. The government you so despise? They approved it and so here we are.' Mr. White smiled once more as he explained again, 'But you can still walk out of here if you do to yourself what you forced those women to do. If you cut yourself, and I mean properly cut yourself... You can leave a free man and we won't ever see you again. Although, I'll be honest, you may want to stay away from your management team because I don't think they have your best interests at heart.'

Nate just laid there, unsure as to what to say or whether to believe any of this. Was it really his manager who made all this come to fruition? Could he have done that? He knew - without Mr. White explaining further - that the answer was yes.

'Do you know how painful a paper cut is? Imagine that little piece of card slice through the skin of those pussy lips. Little rips which whilst not life threatening would certainly be uncomfortable for weeks after the event. You asked them to do that. You asked them to rip their skin open for you and now - to balance it out - I am asking you to do the same for us. Although, you should thank me because I don't have a piece of card. I just had a knife. A knife would take less effort. It would be quicker. A couple of slices to show you're sorry and you can go. How is that not fair for what you've put people through? How am I being unreasonable? Unless, of course, you want to die here in which case just give me the nod and - I'll do it. We will fuck with you some more and then, we will finish up by killing you when you can take no more. So what's it to be?'

'Permission to talk?'

'A yes or no answer.'

'You've got me wrong,' Nate said.

'That doesn't sound like a yes or no answer.' He looked to one of his colleagues and ordered him, 'Pull his tongue from his mouth whilst I get the knife.'

'Wait!' Nate shouted. 'I'm not who you think I am!'

His outburst was enough for Mr. White to momentarily pause in his tracks.

'Oh?'

'Please. I'm not who you think I am.'

'You're not Nate Nasty?'

'I am not… That's not me.'

'Oh really? Okay. Thirty seconds. Explain.'

Part Fifteen
My Name Is Nigel

Nate spoke as clearly as he could given his fear, the pain he was in and the drugs flowing through his blood. 'I was singing karaoke in a bar when Steven Gibson saw me. I was doing a song by the *Sex Pistols* and really going for it. I was running around the stage, jumping around, screaming at the top of my lungs. The rest of the people in the bar were loving it and getting into it. When I was done, Steve Gibson approached me saying he was a manager and that he could see great potential in me. I thought he was joking. I thought it was a prank but he gave me a card. I'm an estate agent. Or I was an estate agent. A dull estate agent in a job that paid the bills but I hated and here was this guy offering me the world. Why would I not call him up and chat to him? He invited me to his office and I went with no expectations. By the time I left, he'd offered me a deal. Lead singer of a punk band he was putting together. I still couldn't believe it and even joked that I wasn't the type of person who'd look good fronting such a band. He told me not to worry about that. He would deal with it all. All we needed was a good publicist. Someone to leak fabricated stories to the press on our behalf. Stories which would make me sound more than I was. I wasn't actually doing what they said I was doing! I was mostly at home, or in hiding so as not to be spotted out. That's why the rape case was thrown out. Because I didn't do it! We could prove I had never even met that woman! That's why it was so easy to get it thrown out. And the story of Dean M. Watts in the bar? The guy I supposedly glassed? You said it yourself - you couldn't find him because he didn't exist! We made him up! We made the whole story up. And Becca Ross? I did meet her. I own up to that and spending the night with her but we actually spent the night watching old black and white movies on my projector. We kissed but that was it. She was paid not to say what really happened! She even signed a non-disclosure agreement! When she died, it was nothing to do with me and I was devastated because I liked her! I never once treated her without respect! I treated her like a Queen the whole time we were together. I treat everyone good… The stories you hear, they're all just to get people talking and keep the band in the papers! That's it! My name isn't Nate! My name is Nigel! Nigel Nateson and I was an estate agent!' He added, 'Oh and the video? There is no such video! Again the information was leaked. That's all it takes. Leak it out and let the lies spread like wildfire. That's why no one even knows what concert it was a part of and yet, if it really happened, you think it wouldn't have been captured on mobile phones or the like? It's all lies! And they're lies made by Steven Gibson!' He stopped talking and took several deep breaths as the panic continued to set in. He said quietly, 'I've never hurt anyone.'

When Nate stopped talking, a silence fell over the room. Eventually Mr. White shrugged. He said, 'Whatever your plans with your manager, clearly they're not working anymore and he has a lot invested in you. He needs to make that money back so, here we are. It's a tricky predicament, if what you are saying is true, but - at the end of the day - we have been paid for a service. Now do you promise what you're saying is true?'

Nate nodded. 'Yes! I swear to God!'

'Well then, in that case, there's little point in having you cut yourself. After all, if you didn't make those women cut themselves then it is unfair of us to force you to do it too. Although obviously we're too late for the cum-eating and the eyeball and I've sorry about that.' Mr. White paused a moment as he contemplated the situation they found themselves in. He added, 'There's little point in having you cut yourself but, at the same time, it's entirely necessary that we do go through with it.'

'Why?!'

'Because of the lies. Just because I know the truth. We know the truth. The people out there don't. They still believe you're the character you and your manager have created and so... We can't have them walking around thinking it is acceptable to behave like that. So, truth or not, an example has to be set.' Mr. White added, 'I'm afraid to say, Nigel, that you are that example.'

'Please.... WE CAN TALK ABOUT THIS...'

Mr. White shook his head slowly from side to side. 'Now, Nate, did we not warn you about speaking out of turn?'

Viewer Discretion Is Advised

Two gloved fingers pulled Nate's tongue from his mouth as the camera whirred. Nate is trying to talk but - with his tongue gripped so tight - the words aren't being formed.

A pair of rusty scissors enter the shot. They're open. They slide over the tongue so that one blade is above and one is below.

The camera zooms in closer still. The camera shakes visibly due to the extremes of which it is zoomed in and the unsteadiness of the operator's hands.

The scissors slowly close, cutting through the tongue in the process. A sound similar to slicing through a raw piece of steak with a knife's serrated blade. Less effort required with regards to the cutting.

Nate's screams intensify.

[VOLUME DOWN]

Blood gushes the moment the tongue is cut. Dark red in colour, it fills Nate's mouth and pools there, trickling out over the edges and down the sides of his face as he squirms around held - again - in place by hands on his head.

The camera follows the now severed tongue as it is pulled from the mouth. The viewers at home get to watch the tongue get rolled into a ball, held only in place by the fingers rolling it. If they release the tongue, it would surely unfold out flat once more.

Nate continues to cry out.

The camera follows the balled-tongue as it is pushed into the socket where once there had been an eyeball.

[VOLUME UP]

A squelching noise. Three fingers fiddling in a moist pussy once more. Wet. Sloppy. Another example? Someone rolling warm saliva around on the inside of their cheek.

The fingers release the rolled-tongue and, as much as it can, it unrolls in the socket stretching the socket like a thick dick stretching open a tight cunt. The socket holds the remainder of the tongue as a less-than-perfectly formed ball.

[STATIC]

Nate's face fills the shot. He is screaming. The tongue is still held in place in his eye socket. There is vomit and dried cum around his mouth and on the table beneath his head.

[STATIC]

A circumcised penis is in the shot. The camera is zoomed in. It looks more impressive than it really is. A razor blade enters the shot and presses against the shaft of the cock. The slightest of pressure opens the skin up and blood trickles out. The razor lifts away and comes back into the shot and presses against another part of the prick. Again, it presses against the shaft with little weight behind it but - still - the shaft opens and more blood spills out. The razor leaves the shot.

Two fingers enter the shot and hold the cock steady.

Tweezers come into the shot and push into one of the small incisions. They twist and turn, opening the flesh a little more in the process. The thickness of the skin is visible. Pink either side of white for a split second before it disappears under a pool of blood.

The tweezers are pulled from within. Clamped in their mouth - a purple stringy vein. As the tweezer moves upwards from the shot, the cock moves with it as the vein continues to break free.

A knife enters the shot. The purple vein is cut.

[STATIC]

Nate is unconscious. His skin is wet. His complexion is pale. A hand enters the shot. Gripped between its fingers are some smelling salts. They go under Nate's nose and slowly, he comes around. The hand moves from the shot. Another hand enters, holding a knife.

The knife pushes into the side of Nate's neck and pops out the other side. His eyes are wide. His mouth open and gasping for air that doesn't come. The knife is pulled from his neck. There is a jettison of blood from both holes. His Adam's apple pulses as he continues to gasp. More blood is seen, starting to pool in the bottom of his already bloody mouth.

Panic on his face.

[SCREEN PAUSES]

'And the main news again; the lead singer of *The Black Room Manuscripts* has been found dead; his body tortured beyond recognition. Along with the body, a note was found stating the infamous punk singer got only what he put others through.'

A newsreader looked coldly into the camera as though the death of Nate meant entirely nothing to her. She shuffled some papers from the desk she sat at and then said to camera, 'And now, a look through to this weekend's weather…'

The bar's television screen turned to black as the bartender killed the power to it.

'Jesus - that was fucking intense,' he said as he turned back to the bar and the patrons standing there; all of whom had been watching the broadcast.

'Karma,' one person said. 'You're an asshole to people, people are an asshole to you. He got what was deserved.'

'You really think it's that though?' Another person was heard to say, 'I heard the government had him killed.'

'They can do that?'

'Fucking A they can. You mess with them… You're a big enough dick, they'll fucking take you down. We won't ever know it's the government but, it's them.'

'So why is Justin Bieber still alive?'

'Ain't no governments wants to accept responsibility for the little prick.'

'Fair.'

Back to the tape they'd seen. 'I'd heard it was something to do with his latest album. Apparently some of the songs in it are so fucking anti-establishment…'

'Aren't they always?'

'No - apparently he *really* went to town on them this time. I heard this was their answer. Fuck him up and shut him up.'

'Well, he's been shut up. That's a fucked up way to go.'

'Fucking tell me about it.'

'I'm sorry to bother you,' a voice approached the men at the bar from behind where they stood. It belonged to Steven Gibson.

The men turned to face him.

'We help you?'

'Before the news… I heard you up on the karaoke… You got a real good voice.'

'Taking the piss, mate?'

'No. You've got natural talent…'

Steven reached into his pocket for his business card.

Author Bio

Matt Shaw is the author of over 200 published works. As well as appearing in a number of anthologies, Matt's work has been translated into French, German, Korean and Japanese. His work has also been adapted into graphic novels and - more recently - film.

Having successfully crowdfunded a feature film, in 2018 Matt Shaw adapted his best-selling novel MONSTER into a screenplay (with Shaun Hutson acting as script consultant) and then went on to direct it himself. The film starred Rod Glenn, Tracy Shaw (*Coronation Street*), Laura Ellen Wilson and Danielle Harold (*Eastenders*). Having broken his "film cherry", Matt is currently producing two more feature films - one an original piece which he wrote for screen (*Next Door*) and a second based on another of his novellas (*Love Life*).

Matt tours both the UK and the US on regular book signings but - if you're unable to get to where he is -

there is also a store where you can purchase signed merchandise direct from him over on ETSY. Simply look up *The Twisted World of Matt Shaw* where you'll find exclusive downloads, his infamous *DeadTed* bears and more…

Want to stay up to date with Matt? He can be found on Twitter, Instagram and Facebook. There is also a fan club which has exclusive stories, early reads, behind the scenes information and a whole lot more - available on Patreon!

Lightning Source UK Ltd.
Milton Keynes UK
UKHW010626170320
360479UK00001B/109